JOCKO

A Long Way from Home Down Under

Waymon Lefall

Copyright © 2014 Waymon E. Lefall
All rights reserved
First Edition

PAGE PUBLISHING, INC.
New York, NY

First originally published by Page Publishing, Inc. 2014

ISBN 978-1-62838-503-8 (pbk)
ISBN 978-1-62838-504-5 (digital)

Printed in the United States of America

Growing up in Dallas, Texas in the '30s –'40s, there was this little black statue on white folks lawns everywhere. During my employment cutting grass throughout the white neighborhoods, we would often come upon those little black statues. We could only wonder what they were or what they meant. As we got older we begin to hear bad things about the little black statues. At that point we started to hate the little black fellow standing there with a lantern in his extended right hand. At night, we began to try and destroy the statues through vandalism. We should have known better; we thought that was the way to fight back for the mockery of the little black boy. Little did we know that the little black boy statue meant something great. Older folks never talked about the statue. I guess it was taboo at the time. After serving time in the U.S. Army and getting my honorable discharge, I met a great man by the name of Mr. Earl Koger Sr., who had been studying the history of the little black boy statue. Mr. Koger hired me on to work for his newspaper, *Good News*. After studying and working under Mr. Koger, I learned a great deal about the little black boy statue, known as Jocko Graves. Mr. Koger explained to me how the statue came to be. The story goes something like this:

> During the Revolutionary War, a free Black man named Tom Graves joined George Washington's army. Graves' 12-year-old son, Jocko, wanted to go to war too, but was deemed too young. Undeterred, Jocko went anyway. As Washington was preparing to cross the Delaware River

for the battle of Trenton, he realized he couldn't transport horses by boat, and that his steeds would have to be waiting on the other side. Jocko volunteered to hold the horses and make sure they were ready when Washington's troops arrived. But during the night, Jocko froze to death awaiting the soldiers, never letting go of the reins. His sacrifice spurred the troops into victory, and Washington was so touched by the boy's sacrifice that he erected a statue in Jocko's honor at Mount Vernon. This statue, the story goes, was the precursor to the lawn jockey.

Jocko's story has been told many times before in many ways and details vary from teller to teller. His age fluctuates, as does the side of the river he was standing on. Sometimes he's holding a lantern, sometimes not. But the gist of the story remains the same: Lawn jockeys are not racists' reminders of the days of slavery, but monuments to an American hero. The only problem is that no one can seem to find any record of Jocko Graves, or for that matter, a statue of an African-American boy at Mount Vernon. But LeFall is a believer. He is determined to bring the story of Jocko to the masses through a small child's book he self-published in November, *Legend of Jocko: Hero of the American Revolution*.

With his new children's book, Waymon LeFall wants to change the way people think about lawn jockeys.

"One day everybody will be educated," LeFall says. "And people might feel proud to put Jocko back out there on their lawn, because now he's out there for a reason."

It takes an unlikely man to tell an unlikely story. A third-generation barber born in Dallas, Lefall came to Baltimore in 1966 and opened a chain of barbershops. His shop in Midtown-Edmondson, Lefall and Co. Unisex Hair Salon, has become the cornerstone of the small neighborhood on the city's west side, and LeFall himself has become it's unofficial mayor, advocating for the struggling area and serving as its spokesman. In 1995, *The Sun* ran an article about LeFall's decision to back Mary Pat Clarke over Kurt Schmoke in the mayoral race, and his opinion has been asked on everything from his neighborhood's crime and grime problems to the O.J Simpson trial verdict. LeFall also markets a line of barbecue products and has started *RazorsEdge* magazine, geared towards barbers and beauty salons. The first issue included a lengthy article about LeFall himself.

But LeFall's main passion is Jocko. He originally heard the story from another colorful Baltimore character, Earl Koger Sr., insurance broker, publisher of community newspapers, and author in 1963 of a 32-page children's book called Jocko: A Legend of the American Revolution. Koger's little book was published by Prentice Hall and circulated widely: a copy of it is now held in the collection of the Great Blacks in Wax Museum, which also features a wax figure of the frozen child in its exhibit "And the Little Child Shall Lead Them: Black Youth in the Struggle." But the story of Jocko, like Koger's book, never really caught on.

When Koger died in 1995, LeFall, who worked for one of Koger's newspapers and considered him a mentor, vowed to keep the story of Jocko alive. "I was really under his wing," he says. "We were like father and son working together."

In 2000, LeFall found an old lawn jockey at a junkyard. A few months later, a friend sent him another. This one was hollow, so LeFall decided to use it as a mold to create his own Jocko statues. He brought it to a local foundry and had aluminum and bronze figures made. But he wasn't content with the minstrel-like images of the traditional lawn jockeys.

"When I found Jocko, he had red lips, white eyes, and a black face," he says. "And I don't know of anyone that has red lips, white eyes and a black face. So we took Jocko and gave him some life, gave him some meaning, gave him an identity as a 12-year old boy during that time." LeFall convinced longtime friend and painter Matthew "BayBay" Williams to hand paint the sculptures.

But the sculptures didn't sell well. "I just think that Jocko was given a disservice," LeFall says. "We as Black people always thought Jocko was a negative. That's why a lot of Jockos were stolen off lawns. They were destroyed. People had to be educated about Jocko because there was such an uproar over the past, the negatives of Jocko."

So in the spring of 2003, with the help of Editor Carolyn Gaither-Ellis (whose company, Productions Supreme printed the book) and illustrator Gary Phillips, LeFall began putting together a children's book of his own. "I still felt that I wasn't educating the people enough," he says. "I had to go another step."

Geared toward children ages 5 to 12, the 22-page book contains LeFall's version of the Jocko tale, borrowing heavily from Koger. "But when [Washington] landed and approached the precious steeds," LeFall writes toward the conclusion of the book, "he discovered that they were not secured to a stump but held by the little Negro boy, Jocko, who was covered with ice and snow. Jocko had stood all night long, holding the horses for General Washington and had frozen to death."

It ends with a picture of a smiling Jocko statue at Mount Vernon and the words "and a statue of Jocko stepping bravely forward to hold the horses as if saying 'I will', was set upon the lawn."

Still, there are those who dispute the merit of the Jocko story, the lawn jockey, and LeFall's efforts to rescue them from history. To Kenneth Goings, chair of African-American and African Studies at Ohio State University and author of a book about African-American memorabilia called Mammy and Uncle Mose; the lawn jockey cannot and should not be reclaimed.

"There's been other attempts to reclaim other things, like the Mammy cookie jars," Goings says. "I don't think that they're going to be successful. I don't think that they can be reclaimed. They are meant to evoke that old South, grand plantation, *Gone with the Wind,* mythology, and I'm not sure they can evoke anything else."

Goings also doesn't see any historical basis for the tale. "Something like that would have popped up in some primary sources," he says.

The historians at Washington's home, Mount Vernon, agree. In a 1987 letter to the Enoch Pratt Free Library, Mount Vernon librarian Ellen McCallister Clark wrote that "the story is apocryphal; conveying a message about heroism among blacks during the Revolutionary War and General Washington's humanitarian concerns, but it is not based on an actual incident. Neither a person by the name of Jocko Graves, nor the account of any person freezing to death while holding Washington's horses has been found in any of the extensive records of the period. Likewise, the Mount Vernon estate was inventoried and described by a multitude of visitors over the years and there has never been any indication of anything resembling a 'jockey' statue on the grounds. I have put the story in the category with the cherry tree and silver dollar, fictional tales that were designed to illustrate a particular point."

"It's a true story," insists LeFall, back in his barbershop. "It has been erased. It's not there anymore, but that doesn't mean that Jocko wasn't there, because Jocko is here and he's all over the world."

Joann Martin, co-founder of the Great Blacks in Wax Museum, likewise feels that the lack of documentation doesn't necessarily disprove the Jocko legend, pointing out that much of the documentation of Black history has been lost. But regardless of the factual basis, Martin feels that the story serves a purpose. "Whatever the reality may be- and there's always truth in any story- the important thing for me is that, just as the John Henry legend or the legend of Paul Bunyan or any of those legends, that there's always some kind of moral lesson," Martin says. She also points to the use of lawn jockeys in the Underground Railroad to warn escaped slaves of danger, or to signal a safe house by tying brightly colored fabric to the statue's arm or lighting a lantern in its hands, as other reasons the jockeys should be remembered.

Regardless of the evidence- or lack of it- LeFall has faith in his little American hero. "Jocko is for real," he says. "If you don't believe in Jocko, then ask yourself, where did he come from? And if you can't answer that, believe in something. Believe in Jocko." (Ditkoff 2004)

From Edgecombe Elementary School

Dear Mr. LeFall,

Your book is an excellent resource for children. It serves as a historical resource that will teach young and old about a historical figure that is an American Legend. The added bonus was your book reading and signing at our school. You shared your wonderful story of Jocko with the entire student body, which also enlightened both teachers and staff of a long hidden historical fact. Now when anyone from our school sees a lawn jockey, they can share the history of this memorable piece of art! I am sure that your book will be an excellent teaching tool in American History.

Stories of Jocko from Around the USA

You Decide (newspaper clip)

This statuette is one of two removed from the Crewe Railroad Museum following complaints from several people. They had once been used by a former Norfolk & Western engineer to signal that he was out on a run. A museum committee recently decided to give them back to the person who donated them.

Email from: W. Wade Walker- Town Manager/Town of Crewe, Virginia

Mr. LeFall:

Well, the saga of our two Jocko's finally came to a rather disappointing end. The Railroad Museum opted to remove the statues and return them to their original owner rather than face the negative publicity generated by local media and citizens during open town council meetings. While no one ever really came forward officially, the museum was advised the statues were offensive to some. Rather than offend anyone, they decided to have them removed.

Many feel this was most unfortunate and the figures should have been exploited with plaques explaining their story, but just like most small towns, it got out of hand and in the best interest of keeping the peace, the decision was made for removal. As you know, the original owner once again has them proudly displayed in her front yard, as they have been for many years. She brought and showed me the book you sent her and I am sure she is very glad to have it on hand when someone asks her about the statues.

I appreciate your correspondence and should you ever be in our area, I am sure the owner would be honored to have you visit her statues. They are very well preserved and she has always maintained them in top condition.

Thank you again, and I wish you well with your passion for Jocko!

Baltimore, Maryland

Good morning,

My intrigue with Jocko started when Orrin some time ago came home with a T-shirt and a stuff bear from your community event. He told me all about his history with you, and all of the adventures you are involved in and have gone through. Orrin gave me a copy of the book, and instantly to my amazement, I became so enlightened with the history of Jocko. I always enjoy stories of untold African American history. Reading about Jocko has added more knowledge to a part of my history as told through my grandfather. My grandfather was a little upset that my mother was involved with a Greek man, therefore, wanted to make sure that his grandchildren know about our roots in the South and North Carolinas, and African Americans contributions to the world.

    I had a stroke in November of last year right after Thanksgiving; therefore, my memory is a little shock. I can still remember a few things. During my recovery, I read the Jocko book again, and simply was so intrigue with his story, and your quest to make his story known.

    I have told my children about Jocko's story, and the impact he made in American history. They stated that they never heard of him through their schools, and I told them that this is an untold story, and that most school books are created by whites, and most of African American accomplishments go unrecognized.

    As I told you before, I was teased as a little girl because of my race background that is why my grandfather wanted us to know our backgrounds and where we came from. My cousin who is an Enoch Pratt Library director for the Northeast district told us African American folk stories and poetry, I loved to hear these stories, and like to read about them. Reading the Jocko book has added some knowledge that was once unknown to me, and I really appreciate the opportunity to assist you in any way, shape, or form to get your story out.

I want to thank you for including me in your dream, and inspirations with Jocko, and I will try my best to help get his story out.

If you would like to ask me anything else, please feel free to do so.

Always a Pleasure,
Trina McCullough

Hello Mr. LeFall,

My husband works for Cumberland Foundry in Cumberland, RI. While cleaning out their patterns, the workers came across one of Jocko. The pattern found is a loose 4 piece pattern.

The Figure, when made are approximately 26 inches tall, made of cast iron, there is also a base

that he stands on. There is no pattern for a lantern. Normally, these loose castings are bolted or welded together.

In researching the history of this figure, we came across your website. We thought you would be interested in knowing that some of the workers, who are African American, thought

the figure was racist when until they read the history of Jocko. We agree with you that more people need to know the history of this statue.

I am a fifth grade teacher; the Revolutionary War is in our curriculum. I am purchasing your book to read aloud to my students. I would appreciate if you could autograph it.

Thank you for your time,
Lisa and Jim Murphy

Email from: Walt Matthews/Commercial Casting Sales Manager/TB Wood's, Inc.

Dear Mr. LeFall,

I am writing in response to the phone call that Dan Szekalski made about you possibly giving a talk at one of our monthly meetings of the Chesapeake Chapter of the American Foundry Society. We are Foundry men and vendors from different areas of the Foundry Industry. As Chairman of the Chesapeake Chapter, I am extending the invitation for you to speak, if you are agreeable please reply to this email. The Jocko Statue and its history would be a very interesting topic to be presented. We have monthly meetings starting on October 21, 2010. It is the beginning of our schedule so pretty much any month we meet is open at this point. So if this date suits your schedule please let us know by Monday, June 28, 2010. The chapter is very interested in the history behind this casting from its beginning. We give presenters a meal and the full attention of the group for a 20 to 30 minute time frame. We hold our meetings in and around the Hanover, PA area. We would let you know the location of the actual meeting place once we have it finalized. I will be awaiting your response. I want to thank you for the interest in speaking to our group.

Sincerely,
Walt Matthews
Commercial Casting Sales Manager
TB Wood's, Inc.

Email from: Walt Matthews/ Commercial Casting Sales Manager/TB Wood's Inc.

Hi Waymon,

We all would like to thank you for the opportunity to hear the history of Jocko. It was enjoyed by all. I am sorry I did not respond sooner but I am traveling on business in New York and Massachusetts. I wish you luck with your investigation looking for the original pattern for the Jocko Statue. I feel it was a great meeting.

Thanks again,
Walt Matthews
Chairman AFS
Chesapeake Chapter

Press Release

The Legend of Jocko & the Historic Trip Down Under

Release Date: December 6, 2009

Who: Waymon LeFall, Author

What: Journey to Maitland, Australia to research the statue of Jocko placed in the town

When: December 8-16, 2009

Why: To research and tell the Legend Story of Jocko to the people of Australia

Where: Maitland, South Australia

Through history and time, many known facts about African American's contributions have gone unwritten in American history books. Many authors have proclaimed the rights to write about unknown facts of African Americans, but one author made it a personal quest to tell the tale of one young boy's remarkable bravery. Famed barber, Waymon LeFall brings attention to an unknown, but extraordinary story of young Jocko, The First African American Child Hero.

Baltimore barber turned author Waymon LeFall brings what he calls a missing piece of African American history to light in his children's book, "The Legend of Jocko, Hero of the American Revolution." His book shares the little known inspirational story of a 12-year-old African American boy named Jocko who sacrifices his life for our country.

Now in the process of running his successful barbershop, LeFall also wrote a book about in his opinion, the First Afro-American child hero. He wrote the book, "The Legend of Jocko", the small African American boy that was once recognized as a racist object. LeFall hopes that his story will change the racist artifact into a symbol of African American pride. From book signings, school appearances, and community events, LeFall strives to provide key knowledge of Jocko's bravery to the world.

The statue of Jocko is not only sat upon lawns in the United States, but after many years of coming to Jocko's aid, LeFall soon discovered that the Legend of Jocko is truly a legend of its own rights in the land down under. This discovery was brought to LeFall through a common interest by Jack, a native of Australia. Through constant emails conversations, LeFall will soon find out how inspirational the story of Jocko has become to the small town of Maitland, Australia.

Intrigue with LeFall's story of triumph, Jack has invited LeFall to take a trip to the historic Maitland, Australia, to speak to the people of this small but significant city about the legend of the little Negro boy who stands so proudly in front of one of the neighboring stores. LeFall plans to make this historic journey to Maitland on November 8, 2009. On his trip, LeFall plans to explain his opinion of the legend of Jocko, and describes why it is important for him to let the world know of the unknown tale of bravery by young Jocko. To let the people know that this small Negro statue that sits in front of his store, is truly a remarkable, braved hero of the American people and its history.

Dear Mr. LeFall,

What a wonderful site you have honoring Jocko! Our family has had a "lawn jockey" for over 80 years. It was my mom and dad's at their ranch and now it is mine. We live in a small, rural, predominantly white community. Not too long ago my granddaughter's friend came to the house. He asked her, "Emma, why is there a statue of a small black man in your yard?" Thankfully, Emma was able to tell him the story of Jocko as it had been related to me when I was a young girl.

So congratulations to you. It is a heart warming story of an American and so important to the history of our black citizens. I'm going to order your book today.

God bless and best wishes,
Linda Chambers
Gardnerville, Nevada

Part Two

We Began Our Journey Down Under Maitland, Australia In Search of Jocko

Subject: Re: Jocko Legend
Date: 9/14/2009 9:48:08PM
From: jacks_management@hotmail.com
To: lefallandco@aol.com

Hi,

I was just wondering if you would still have copies of the book (publication) that was written about Jocko Graves. I am interested in purchasing a copy of the book- (story)

 In Australia a statue of Jocko is still around. One I have attached and is located here in Australia (where I am) - and has been here since 1860's, when it was brought out from the US by iron-mongers.

 I got interested in the statue, as I remember as a kid first seeing the statue stand in the street of town, where it still is today. In recent years I have written a song about the little statue telling the legend behind it, which I will be publishing a sheet music here in Australia.

Jack

Hi Jack,

Instead of sending the book, why not, I bring the book? Which would allow me to meet you and see Jocko for myself and tell the story of the Little fellow to the people of Australia.

Sent: Friday, Sept 25, 2009
Subject: Jocko

Hi Waymon,

I'm just south of Sydney, NSW, so Sydney is a major city where the international airport is located. The place where the statue (Jocko) is, is about 2.5 hours north of Sydney…there is flight there from Sydney as well, as a train ride.

If you are planning on coming out- the best time would be November. I will have to get accommodations in the town where Jocko is (hotel room) for a couple nights for myself as well.

What are your plans? Traveling with someone to Australia? Re: Sydney and where Jocko is- I can show you around the place- particularly the City. I don't drive, but there are public transports.

I was going to email this morning- letting you know that in my research I have found 2 more Jocko statues that were in South Australia- however in 1987 they were decapitated, as some folks in the town wanted them out, because they believe the statues exploited black slavery era. Their local museum didn't want them either. I dare say they didn't know the history-and saw them to offensive. It's a shame as they were brought out to Australia 1873, and are of historical value. I have information about those 2 statues- and you are welcome to read about them when you come out.

Luckily- the one previously told you about, is still standing on the footpath of the street, the local council (so I believe) have recently given him a fresh coat of paint.

I was about 6 years old or so- when I first seen the statute, now 30 years later it is still standing there, where it has been for the past 130 years or so.

Everything is well over this side of the world. I am also compiling a small book re: the black boy statue and its history in Australia (also the South

Australian ones) with the legend behind them as well. Don't know when that will be published.

I have also started writing another song regarding another African American hero (I think that would be a word I would use) – Henry O. Flipper. I love true stories, whether its Australian, British or American.

Well it's great to hear from you again.

Cheers,
Jack

From J.P. Management <Jack>
Subject: Jocko
Date: Sat, Sept 26, 2009

Hi Waymon,

Let me work out the dates- when I see the people involved (ie: historical society, etc.). If you can arrive in Sydney on November 26 (Wednesday), I think this would be ok, however, I will confirm this with you by October 7.

As I said previously, if they are not interested- then I will definitely get the local paper to do a front page story and get them to take a pic of you with the statue. This way you can tell the story and it will be published, for all to read.

Might even get Sydney paper and a couple magazines to run a feature story. At least this way, the story about Jocko (legend behind the hitch posts) will be told, etc.

I dare say tomorrow (Monday) or Tuesday, the package may arrive, soon as it does I will e-mail you. If it does come before Friday, I will head up to the Valley and show them the details, etc. and see if they are interested.

As I said, if they are not, then I will line up the local newspaper and magazines to do articles while you are out here re: the hitching post. I was told that the one here could be the eldest surviving hitching post- built 1860's that looks like a little boy.

Will let you know soon as the package arrives.

Cheers
Jack

GOOD NEWS—For Starters!!!

I have contacted the towns' newspaper and they would love in doing story with you, re: Jocko. They were pleased that I contacted them. They are proud of their famous black boy statue. They will be able to take a pic of you and the statue for the story as well.

I have put together a media release to get a couple magazines and other large papers to do an article as well, as the little black boy statue is one of Australia's famous icons since 1866- naturally originally from the US.

Next Monday, October 5 is a public holiday, so I don't think I will hear anything back (on a decision) until October 9, soon as I hear anything- will let you know.

Cheers
Jack

From: Jack
Subject: Sydney
Date: Wed, Oct 7, 2009

Hi,

Yeah if you book a hotel/motel in Sydney CBD you'll be pretty much Central to everything:

- * Opera House on the Quay
- * Centre Point Town which looks over Sydney (Pitt Street mall) and many other things there.

If you arrive in Sydney on Tuesday November 10, I will catch up with you on Wednesday evening, November 11 as I live south about 2 hours Sydney- then up north to the Valley on Friday morning, November 12.

Not sure where I will stay 1 night in Sydney yet, hopefully it's not too far where you will be staying.

Where the Jocko statue is- is about 2.5 hours north of Sydney.

Maitland, NSW is the town where the statue is, on the main street. There are accommodations in Maitland, and also in East Maitland. I'm not sure yet, but I may be staying at the Hotel- across from Jocko statue…it's been years since I last stayed at that hotel- so not sure how good the accommodation is there.

Cheers
Jack

From: Jack
Subject: Interviews
Date: Thu, Oct 8, 2009

Hi

I have 2 interviews so far- when you come out to Maitland:

- * Local Newspaper
- * Local News- TV interview

They are interested in the story being told about the black boy statue— which of course is Jocko. Although you will not be paid for it, at least the story will be told.

There is one more- I will try and get- which is Australia wide. Will let you know. The TV crew is going to call me on November 10 to see what day we will be in Maitland.

Your story will be read and heard by many

Cheers
Jack

Monday, October 12, 2009

Hello Trina,

You have done a wonderful job getting press release together, I can't thank you enough. God knows what he is doing bringing us together with Jack and the people of Australia on Jocko's behalf. I thank you and God bless you. Talk to you soon, my plate was full for a moment but now it's half full. It's a good feeling.

Thanks,
Waymon

From: Trina McCullough
To: Waymon LeFall
Subject: Jocko
Date: Mon, Oct 12, 2009

Hello Mr. LeFall,

YOU ARE SO WELCOME!! I am glad that you like the press release. They say that God works in mysterious ways, therefore, everything happens for a reason.

There is one more exciting news I have for you. I may have a companion joining you on your trip. I have been working with the news producer from

WJZ for some time now. I told him all about you and your trip to Australia. He was very impress with the story, and may contact you to see if they can do a story about your trip. He stated that he will get back with me sometime this week to let me know who will cover the story. But, I wanted to get your permission first before I give them the go ahead.

Get back with me to let me know.

God Bless you and I will be praying for you on your trip to Australia.

Remember, take plenty of pictures. I can use them to do some things for you.

Always a Pleasure,
Trina

I am trying to get a magazine interested in doing an article as well- so far no luck.

When we arrive in Maitland- we'll book into the hotel, and then go and see the Jocko statue. On the same day you will also be interviewed. There are 2 Jocko statues in Maitland- the original and the duplicate- one is standing on the footpath the other in the government building. They did a replica a few years back, just in case something happens to the one standing on the footpath.

We can see the second statue as well, if you would like.

My relations are from the area- that's where my mother grew up and her family line has been in the Hunter Valley just as long as the statue '1865'.

So I do know the area well. So when we arrive, straight to Hotel- then head down the street to see Jocko. Two days before you arrive I will contact the papers to confirm a time with them to do the story. They'll come out to the statue and may take a pic of you with the statue and get your story then.

It has been briefly told re: the history of Jocko, but seems that you are the author of the children book etc., it would be better if the story is told by you.

Waymon, I honestly believe a movie of Jocko would do well, it may also cause some controversy, particularly among the African Americans, but if told correctly- by using the hitching post in movie and not the lawn-jockeys, I'm sure it will do well. I can use the actual Jocko-statue (hitching post) to tell the story.

I will let you read what I have already completed, however it could take 18 months or more to get something like this complete…as it is also dealing with facts re: Washington and the Revolutionary War.

Here's part of the story.

Synopsis- Copyright 2009

A new business opens in West Maitland NSW 1866, they are Ironmongers from USA. They set up store in West Maitland making and selling goods. Alongside their store they build a small shed- where the blacksmith would work, the blacksmith- is an elderly African American age 68 known only as 'Old Jack' who was brought out with the company as a free man because of his profession as blacksmith. ('Old Jack' born 1797, was told the story of Jocko by his own father- and he tell the story to a 12yr old Australian boy)—then the scene goes back to 1776-when it all happened.

That is main structure- built around the Jocko statue when it arrived in Australia. I will show you the rest when you arrive.

Cheers,
Jack

From: Jack
To: Waymon LeFall
Subject: Maitland
Date: Mon, Oct 19, 2009

Hi Waymon,

Thursday morning- we would have to leave central station at 7:15am arrives in Maitland 11:30am, if going by train. Where you will be staying is only a few meters away from Central Station.

The TV reporters would like to do the story with you re: Jocko legend- virtually soon as we get into Maitland around mid-day- so it can be shown on local TV Thursday night.

The same day we can organize the paper to do the story as well.

The accommodation in Maitland is taken care of, soon as we arrive we'll head to the hotel, drop off stuff, freshen up and getting ready for the interviews.

Jack

From: Jack
To: Waymon LeFall
Subject: Jocko
Date: Wed, Nov 4, 2009

Hi

Yesterday (Wednesday) I had a phone call from the local TV news people- they thought you were in Maitland today, that's show that they are very interested in the story of Jocko.

When you come out could you please bring one of the caps you have 'Jocko' written on it, will pay you when we meet. I should have here- a key ring with the Maitland's black boy hitching post on it you are welcome to that- as remembrance of your trip to Maitland, etc.

A hotel- in High Street, where we'll be staying for the night in Maitland, is just across the way of the black boy statue. Being a country hotel it's not a 5 star or anything like that, I booked it as it was right in Maitland (so we don't have to walk far)- and it's close to shopping center- and Jocko and it's only for 1 night (Thursday, November 12).

Well- have a good and safe trip out- and will meet up with you Wednesday afternoon (sometime around 2pm).

Cheers
Jack

From: Jack
To: Waymon LeFall
Date: Wed, Nov 25, 2009

Hi Waymon

I had a phone-call yesterday from an 86 year old man about 4 hours north Maitland, it was his great grandfather who had bought the Maitland's black boy from Maitland's Iron Mongers in 1892 (almost 30yrs after it arrived in Maitland), and placed it in front of his shop, in the place where he still stands today.

    He is going to send a few early photos of the statue pre 1930's and other articles, so all the info is slowly but gradually coming together.

Jack

Hi

It seems that Maitland's Black Boy will be getting a plaque after all, according to Council, who only just realized the story about Jocko- unbelievable… It took them until March this year…they got it wrong, it wasn't 1866 re: the tobacconist in Maitland- can't wait to release my book.

    At least the black boy gets noticed etc… here's what was said in the papers:

Story of 'little black boy' told

Briony Snedden
18, March, 2010

He has been a symbol of Maitland for 144 years but few know the story behind the city's "little black boy". That will change with a Maitland City Council initiative to relate the

JOCKO: A LONG WAY FROM HOME DOWN UNDER

tale of "Jocko's" role in the American War of Independence, and how he come to be stationed on High Street.

Cr Phillip Penfold came up with the idea for a panel about the significance of the statue displayed with a replica of the "little black boy" in the foyer of Maitland City Council's administrative building.

It was installed yesterday. The council is also investigating the cost of a plaque for the original statue that stand near the corner of Church Street.

"I was born and bred in Maitland and I never knew the story behind the statue," Cr Penfold said.

Legend has it that Jocko was a 12-year-old boy who froze to death in wintry conditions when guarding horses for General George Washington during the Patriots' war against the British.

Maitland's "Jocko" was a gift to a tobacconist in High Street, who donated it to the city in 1866.

From: Jack
To: Rural Press
Subject: Attn: Letter to the Editor
Date: Fri, 28 May 2010

Hello, Rebecca Berry and Staff @ Maitland Mercury News

My name is Waymon Lefall, Author of The Legend of Jocko, I was pleased to hear that the Black Boy will be getting a name plate from the City Council, to show his deeds of December 25, 1776 while holding horses for George Washington at the Delaware River crossing and froze to death while doing so. I would love to see this take place or some pictures of the event.

God gave me the task of putting Jocko in the fore front over 30 years ago and now look at him; God brought Jocko to my attention in the Great City of Maitland, Australia. Never in my wildest dream did I think I would be able to visit Australia to see Jockos, God is good.

My host and good friend Jack Paten and family of Maitland were very gracious to me, The Belmore Hotel staff, the food and service was the greatest. The article the Maitland Mercury News wrote about me and Jocko, words cannot express, we thank you all.

Thanks,
Waymon Lefall, Baltimore, USA
Author

From: Jack
To: Waymon Lefall
Subject: Attn: Letter to the Editor
Date: Thu, May 27, 2010

No worries- will let you know if they publish it, I am sure they will- in the sec of Letters to the Editor'

It is great that they acknowledge him…as through its history here in Australia- Maitland council and other business's in Maitland had made millions out of him- selling spoons, stickers, if there were anything that they could put him on- to make a dollar- they did it for 40 years or so- as he was a tourist attraction for Maitland.

Now it's time to give him some credit and have the story about him imprinted…for generations to come to read

Cheers
Jack

Australian Men Talking to Jocko before going to war

"Dressed statue", many times while on a spree, the Soldiers had gathered around the Little Black boy and dressed him up in their uniforms. Mr. McDonald recalled one scene when four soldiers marched up to the hitching post and one of them delivered an oration telling the little black boy they were going off to War and hoping they would be able to do their duty as well as he did his.

Medium: City News Newspaper
State: South Australia
Date: 12-12-90

Black boys head for obscurity
By Wade Pearce

LIFE'S tough, even for a statue.

And when you're a black, headless statue a long way from home, it's even tougher.

Two of Adelaide's most disliked little boys, fitting that description, have developed nerves of steel to withstand more than 10 years of hatred. But after being booed out of parties, hacked and beheaded, the Blackamoor brothers have finally had enough.

The owner of the pair of bronze Blackamoor statues, the Norman family, wants their little boys back. The waist-high statues of black American slave-boys once served as hitching posts outside the Norman family home in Hill St, North Adelaide. Hayes Norman bought the 1881 statues in the US and bequeathed them to Adelaide City Council in 1927. In 1980, an arm was hacked off one of the brightly-painted, bronze figures and dumped in a North Adelaide garden, but was later welded back on. In 1987, the statues were brutally decapitated and despite attempts to recover the heads, including a $2500 reward offer from the council, they have never been found.

The statues went into hiding and their fate sparked a furor within the council about what should be done with them. Anti-racist groups wanted the headless duo out of town, while a few sentimentalists hailed them as a "quaint" part of history. The council wants to wash its hands of the troublesome statues and give them to the Yankalilla District Historical Society. But the Normans aren't convinced they will be safe there and want to bring them home.

The council has hired a sculpture to model new heads for the statues and will soon bid good riddance to the boys, as soon as they get their heads together.

Statues head for museum
By Celia Parker

SA's controversial Blackamoor statues, beheaded in a vicious attach three years ago, will be restored to former glory by Adelaide City Council.

The 1881 bronze statues, which once served as hitching posts outside the Norman family home at 83 Hill St., North Adelaide, will then be handed over to the Yankalilla District Historical Museum for display.

The museum was chosen because of it close proximity to Normanville, named after Adelaide dentist, Dr. Hayes Norman, who bought the statues in the US and had them installed on the pavement.

The statues, which depict two black boys in waiting, have had a troubled "life" since Dr. Norman donated them to ACC in 1927.

Those who viewed the gaily-painted "red-coasted, white breeched" South American slave figures with affection were horrified by the decapitation.

It was the second hacking of the statues.

In 1980 an arm of one of the statues was dumped in a North Adelaide front garden after being hacked off by vandals. It was welded back on.

After the decapitation, ACC hid them in storage, while debate on their future raged.

Some considered them a quaint piece of history. Others, including Councilor Mary Lou Jervis, believed them to be valuable tourist attractions and relics of SA heritage which were worth saving.

Opponents believed them to be offensive and embarrassing, decrying them as, "battered relics and symbols of Deep South slavery".

Dr. Norman's grandchildren described them as, "a passive reminder of a by-gone era," and an 83-year-old woman told stories of adorning one of the statues with her "pinny" and dancing around it with her schoolmates, in her younger days.

The ACC, reluctant about putting the statues on open public display again, opted for Yankailllia.

'Little people' from another country
By E. Allen

I wish to contradict a statement (*The Advertiser*, 17/11/88) about the blackamoor statues being brought to Adelaide from the United States in 1930. This is incorrect, The statues were at North Adelaide early this century.

I am 83 and started school in 1911 at St. Catherine's in Barnard St, North Adelaide, and the statues were in Hill St then. They were used as hitching posts by visitors to the owner of the house.

We children, on our way home to Ovingham, Prospect and North Adelaide, loved the two little statues and every afternoon one would take off her "pinny" and the others dance around the statue.

After a goodbye kiss we moved off for home. We never had thoughts about "racism" or "inferiority" in those days. Those statues were just "little people", children from another country.

Please don't have the two statue destroyed. I still hope their heads are in one piece somewhere and can be returned someday.

From: Town & Country Leader
To: Waymon Lefall
Sent: Mon, Jul 26, 2010
Subject: Hello from Maitland, Australia

Hello Waymon, it is always lovely to hear from you and read your emails. It was a wonderful experience to meet you in Maitland and to record the history of our hitching post boy. He is an icon in our city and his story will always live on thanks to your books. It is wonderful for us to have a connection with the American people and part of their history. Look forward to hearing from you and perhaps seeing you again one day soon. Thank you and best wishes, Rebecca Berry, journalist, Maitland Mercury.

From: J Paten
To: Waymon Lefall
Subject: 1983- Black Boy twin
Date: Wed, Sep 29, 2010

Hey

Just came across a new article dated in 1983- "Black Boy Busker"- Maitland's famous black boy has found himself a living, breathing twin- A 12yr old white boy painted himself black- and wore identical clothes to those of the black boy statue busking alongside the statue… One bloke yelled out to the boy "hey, you're a bit dirty" other people started throwing money from their car towards the boy while he performed near the statue. It was stated one little girl ran up the street and yelling 'Mummy, mummy, he's come alive'- (obviously talking about 'Jocko').

Jack

From: J Paten
To: Waymon Lefall
Date: Sat, Dec 11, 2010

Hi Waymon,

How's is all going?
As you know (world news) that Oprah is in Australia… and wasn't here less than 24 hours and was already causing a debate here. Her production people, told a shop over here, to pull down the little golliwog dolls, as they are deemed too offensive for Oprah… this is unbelievable. This sparked a debate over here.

    I am sure Oprah would have seen worse- in the US, I mean (it's not nice to say, and please don't take offense) but it's NOT like we sell over here KKK dolls… which is offensive, even to white people… it's just stupid. The golliwog dolls have been around for years and we had a couple of them back in the 1970s when we were kids.

I was just wondering- if Oprah was visiting Maitland, would her team want the council to remove the famous Black Boy, because it might offend her... I cannot see it happening, the town folk would have something to say about that for sure, so would I for that matter...I mean, this is Australia- she is only a guest. I understand that some things would be deemed offensive to people... but people must move on from the past.

I'm not racist- but I do like the golliwog dolls, I do like the early Negro songs of the 1800's etc. It's all part of history... and of course I can't forget Maitland's famous black boy.

Ah well. Hoping you and yours have a safe Merry Christmas and all the very best for 2011.

Cheers, Jack & Family

To: J Paten
Subject: Re
From: Waymon Lefall]
Date: Sat, 11 Dec 2010

Hello Jack,

I am not at all offended, it's people like Oprah that don't believe in Jocko and grew up with him on white folks lawns all over the place, sometimes we forget where we came from in the Black community. She is still part of the Black community like it or not. The KKK is in her backyard and I have never heard her condemn them, or ask them to stop selling their KKK wares. Wonder if they would stop if she asked, I don't think so. I will not stop promoting Jocko even after death

One Love Mate,
Waymon aka Jocko

Hi Waymon,

Do you know who Ann Chandler Howell, Ph. D- of Baltimore???

Apparently she had contacted Maitland about the black boy statue. Here is part of what she wrote to a Historian in Maitland- in March this year. She seems to be sad that you had to come to Australia to tell the myth (in red).

This was just sent to me today via Maitland in my search. It seems the black boy here has caused some stirring over in your neck of the woods--- and she want to know more.

Cheers,
Jack

From: J Paten
To: Waymon Lefall
Sent: Wed, May 18, 2011
Subject: Re: Ann Howell- Baltimore

No doubt she would have read the articles you wrote on in the net about your visit, and only in March this year, she had to contact the historians of Maitland re: the story etc. Yes, it seems suspect that she contacted the people over here as wants to know the origin of the black boy statue in Maitland. I dunno what other correspondents she had over here that was only one e-mail that was forward onto me today.

Don't worry, it won't derail me, but she for someone of her so-called caliber to contact Maitland, it must be something she truly want to find out about the statue.

Cheers,
J Paten

JOCKO: A LONG WAY FROM HOME DOWN UNDER

To: J Paten
Subject: Ann Howell- Baltimore
From: Waymon Lefall
Date: Wed, 18 May 2011

Hello Jack, well it's the same old thing trying to discredit black people from the beginning of slavery, a Ph. D means she know it all, what a shame. The information I have from around the world from white people who have had a jocko over 200 years and knew the story before I did. Some of these PhD people will say there were no Black Inventors, No Black Jockeys, No Black Air Men, and No Black Horse Soldiers. To bypass me and go all the way to Australia is suspect. Her PhD cannot change the course of history. It is written.

One Love,
Waymon E. Lefall

PS: Sounds like she wanted to say the N---- word, not Sambo, who is Sambo?

Sent: Tuesday, 8 March 2011
Subject: Re: Black Boy Hitching post

Dear Ms. Nicholson,

Your response to my inquiry regarding "Sambo" hitching post is MUCH appreciated **though I am saddened to learn that the myth about the figure has traveled to your shores. There is no evidence to support the notion that this figure represents "Jocko" who was given "life" in a children's book published by Prentice Hall in 1976.** There is nothing in Washington's papers or any of his officers' reports. There are several myths about the night of the crossing and none stand up to reason. One suggests a girl stood on the shore with a lantern to guide the way of the patriots. Since Washington was determined to sneak up on the Brits the cloak of darkness was his best cover. Alas, like Washington chopping down the cherry tree- myths are hard to die.

What I can provide evidence for is the fact that "Sambo" was seen in a catalogue for sale AFTER the American Civil War and there is evidence that it was originally a custom order form an engineer working on a railroad in the southern state of Georgia. Once the order was filled the foundry was free to make copies for sale. It appeared in Robert Wood's post-Civil War catalogue. Thus far there is only evidence that one was shipped to Alabama before the war. There is nothing patriotic about the figure. He was designed to provide a place to attach a horse's rein in the absence of slaves and hired servants. Time changed the function, and it, plus the "jockey" became status symbols before social criticism made them suspect.

However, the date, 1866, associated with your "Sambo" is of significant interest and I would like to untangle the origin of the hitching post. Did Friends & Co. have a business in Newcastle which they expanded to Maitland? Do you have any idea as to the nature of the fountain the figure was associated with or the whereabouts of the other two figures? I ask these questions because the Wood foundry (known as Wood & Perot at the time the hitching post was originally made) also made a line of cast iron fountains. The identification of the fountain, and/or finding the name of the company on other figures would provide the necessary documentation. As things stand there are two competing stories about the origin of the "black boy" and no concert evidence to identify it with the Wood foundry. When Wood went into bankruptcy in 1878 several other companies began to make the hitching posts and a good number of them were made.

One other course for me would be to determine if there are custom house records for the shipment. To search that at the National Archives would require that I knew to whom the casting was shipped and into what port. Would it have been shipped directly or would it have been to a commission merchant? The fact the Fields dealt in iron and other hardware is very encouraging but unfortunately, I have as many questions now as I did at the beginning of this inquiry. I do hope there is more to be learned that will provide answers to the questions.

Regards,
Ann Chandler Howell, Ph.D.

JOCKO: A LONG WAY FROM HOME DOWN UNDER

Hi Waymon

Thank you for that ----

That Ann Howell Ph.D. over where you are- has advertised in Maitland---so it must be getting to here about the Maitland Black Boy. Here is her advertisement again she uses the name "Sambo". We as Australians will be going what the heck is she talking about "Sambo". We don't refer to him as "Sambo"; he is known as Maitland's Black Boy. It's got her thinking on how old the hitching post is.

    I am reconstruction the foundry history Wood & Perot and would like to know if you know when the original "Sambo" hitching posts arrived in Maitland. Can you direct me to a resource which would supply pictures of the little black boy in front of the tobacco shops and any other images of them in town? I would be VERY interested in learning how many were in town.

Posted by Ann Howell

From: J. Paten
To: Waymon Lefall
Subject: Hi
Date: Sat, Oct 13, 2012
Attachments: Maitland_Mascot_Jocko

Hi Waymon,

Thought I would let you know, council has placed a new sign near the black boy statue in their building at Maitland with the words "Maitland's Mascot, Jocko"- with the story about him, along with it. So when people come to the council building, and see the statue there, they can read the story.

    They are hoping to do a plaque similar for the black boy out on the footpath on High Street, so people passing by can read and understand what the Maitland's black boy stands for.

    The picture attached is not a good one, but you can just work out the last word in the heading "Jocko"; the local council is holding the page.

Jack

From: J Paten
Bcc: Waymon Lefall
Subject: Black Boy - $2,500
Date: Sun Nov 4, 2012

Maitland Black boy an 1800's Horse Tether.
$2,500.00 Negotiable

Date Listed: 29/10/2012, Last Edited: 30/10/2013
    A drawn, painted and stitched original tapestry by Maree H Hardy, of a well-loved icon in High Street Maitland
    Teams of horses would be tethered to the copper ring that is still in his hand. His full history is on the internet.
    App. 1 MITRE high, by 600 mm across.

Maitland's Mascot 'Jocko'

Maitland's little black boy statue has been part of the High Street landscape since it was received as a gift by a High Street tobacconist, Friend and Co in 1866.
    The story begins in December 1776 when General George Washington decided to cross the Delaware River to launch a surprise attack on the British forces at Trenton.
    Jocko Graves, a twelve-year-old African-American, sought to fight the Redcoats, but Washington deemed him too young and ordered him to look after the horses, asking Jocko to keep a lantern blazing along the Delaware River so the company would know where to return after the battle.
    Many hours later, Washington and his men returned to their horses who were tied up to Graves, only to find that he had frozen to death with the lantern still clinched in his fist.

Washington was so moved by the young boy's devotion to the revolutionary cause he commissioned a statue of the "Faithful Groomsman" to stand in Graves's honor at the general's estate in Mount Vernon.

By the time the Civil War, these "Jocko" statues could be found on plantations throughout the Southern parts of America including the North Star that pointed freeing slaves to their freedom.

The Jocko statues pointed to the safe houses of the Underground Railroad. Along the Mississippi River, a green ribbon tied to a statue's arm indicated safety: a red ribbon meant danger.

Jocko was a beacon for freedom and is a proud part of Maitland's history.

Whilst the boy below is a replica, the original that was erected by Friend and Co as a hitching post still stands in High Street Maitland today.

Mercury News
Stories REBECCA BERRY
Black Boy Should Be Displayed

"He is holding his pose, he comes from good stock."

With those fond remarks, American author Waymon LeFall proudly studied Maitland's little black boy or hitching post boy.

"It doesn't matter what he is called. He performs the same task- to hold onto the horses."

LeFall visited High Street yesterday and presented the Mercury with two of his children's books about the legend of Jocko, hero of the American Revolution.

He has spent the past 30 years working on Jocko's story and researching the history behind the little boy who froze to death while waiting with George Washington's horses.

Maitland's little black boy has been part of High Street landscape since it arrived here as a gift for a town tobacconist in 1866.

While he is a variation of the original Jocko statue, the meaning behind him is the same and he remains connected to American history, Mr. LeFall said.

"I was so enlightened to find there was a statue like this in Australia," he said.

"They are a rare sight in this county, but they have been placed all over the world and there are many like him in America.

"This statue is revered in America and, through my story telling, people have come to realize that he is a symbol of pride- it is not a racist statue.

"Maitland should place him high, in view of the public. He is something to be proud of and his story should be told. Maitland should always be proud of its connections with the USA."

Jocko steps forward for general

A 12-year-old African American boy named Jocko who sacrificed his life for this country has been an inspiration for Baltimore barber turned author Waymon LeFall.

LeFall describes Jocko as the first American child hero and has brought to life a missing piece of African American history in his children's book The Legend of Jocko, Hero of the American Revolution.

The author discovered Jocko's moment of sacrifice came when George Washington faced defeat during the revolutionary war.

His troops were headed across the Delaware River to Trenton New Jersey to attack the British.

Legend has it that Jocko has crossed the Delaware earlier with volunteer troops and offered to guard Washington's horses so they would be waiting for the general's return.

When Washington returned to Mount Vernon he ordered a sculpture be erected in honor of the young boy stepping bravely forward to hold the horses as if he was saying "I will".

LeFall said replicas that first statue served another purpose years later during the Civil War.

The symbol of Jocko was used in the Underground Railroad to show slaves the way to safety.

LeFall grew up seeing that same image used for lawn sculpture.

He explained the symbol was sadly often misunderstood as a racist decoration.

The author said he was happy to bring Jocko into the light "where he should have been all along".

"Jocko is not only a missing link in African-American history, but in all of history, "LeFall said.

"It is my hope someday that young boys and girls will learn about Jocko in schools. My job is to get Jocko as much recognition as possible."

Lefall said there were many people who would argue that Jocko was a work of fiction, but he challenged the non-believers to prove their case.

FYI

The famous little statue has been standing in several locations in High Street, Maitland for 130 years. He is to thousands of Maitland residents what the Harbour Bridge is to Sydney, the Eiffel Tower is to Paris, and the Statue of Liberty is to New York. Whilst the boy below is a replica, the original still stands in High Street watching the passing parade. He was erected by Friend and Co in 1866 as a hitching post and since that time, he has been decorated in many forms to reflect Maitland's sporting successes over the years. He is an obliging little fellow and an important chapter in the history of High Street, Maitland.

A Long Way From Home

References

Anna Ditkoff, "Jockeying For Respect," *City Paper* (Baltimore, MD), Jan. 21, 2004, accessed December 5, 2013, http://www2.citypaper.com/arts/story.asp?id=5006

Taking of the Children / Jocko on the Pilgrimage

Harbour Bridge

Din Dee & Lefall

Jocko at City Hall

The Opera House

Lefall and friends

Jocko in the Bank

About the Author

Waymon Eugene Lefall was born and raised in Dallas, Texas. He attended Dunbar High, Forth Worth, Texas, a.k.a. stop six.

Waymon was inducted into the U.S. Army and later discharged with honors. He received a A.A. degree from C.C.B. and also his Master Barber License from Baltimore, Maryland. Waymon became a business owner and received his Life Insurance License from Baltimore, Maryland. He later became a teacher and now an author.

Studying journalism under Mr. Earl Koger Sr. brought him to the study of Jocko a.k.a. lawn jockey, The First American Child Hero. Waymon later found Jocko waiting for him in Maitland, Australia. The rest is in this interesting book of History in Fact.

Waymon would like his readers to know that by keeping hope alive, keeping the faith, believing in yourself, and listening to your heart anything can happen. Around each corner turned, something was waiting to connect the dots, he never knew what, but felt something was there, to give up is to lose the dot. Keep the faith.

CPSIA information can be obtained at www.ICGtesting.com
Printed in the USA
BVOW02s1616081115

426211BV00001B/3/P

9 781628 385038